# BLUES GUITAR PHOTO CHORDS

## BY COREY CHRISTIANSEN

*WWW.MELBAY.COM*

# Table of Contents

# Blues Guitar Photo Chords

*Blues Guitar Photo Chords* is a streamlined way for beginners to learn the most commonly used blues chords. Blues guitar can be as simple or difficult as you want. That's one of the great things about it. It can be enjoyed on so many different levels. Of course, this book is focusing on the simple. Very simple. It's been written and organized to help students see the shapes and construction of chords that are commonly used in the blues. Each chord is presented in standard notation, tab, in a chord diagram, and with a photo showing exactly how the chord looks when played on the guitar.

These chords are moveable shapes. This means that by knowing the names of the notes on the fretboard, the shapes presented can be played in virtually every key. The concept of moveable chords is invaluable for all guitarists. It allows us to learn a single shape, and by moving that shape around the fretboard, the chord can be played in every key. All you need to know is where the root (the note that names the chord) is. Page 6 has diagrams that will help you understand the layout of the fretboard. We're not going to show you every chord in every possible key in this book, but if you understand the concept of the moveable chord, you can fill in the missing pieces. Be sure to learn each shape not only in the single key presented, but in all twelve keys. You will not only learn 12 times more chords, but learn the layout of the fretboard. There will be some information on how this is done throughout the book. Also, a few blues progression, which will use these chords have been thrown in so students can see how many of the chords may be used. Have fun.

Corey

# How to Use This Book

Below are explanations for the fretboard diagrams and tab that are used in the book. Standard notation and photos are also used to help students learn what notes are used in each chord and to help them see what the chord literally looks like when played on the guitar.

With the chord diagrams, the vertical lines represent the strings on the guitar, with the first string being on the right. The horizontal lines represent frets, with the first fret being on the top. Dots, or numbers, on the lines show the placement of left-hand fingers. The numbers on, or next to the dots indicate which left-hand finger to use. A diamond may be used to indicate the placement of the root of the chord. **Root** refers to a note which has the same letter name as the chord.

A zero above a string indicates the string is to be played open (no left-hand fingers are pushing on the string). An "X" above a string indicates that string is not to be played, or that the string is to be muted by tilting one of the left-hand fingers and touching the string lightly.

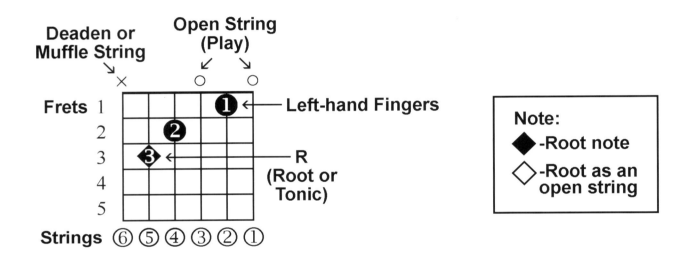

# Tablature

One way of writing guitar music is called tablature. The six horizontal lines represent the strings on a guitar. The top line is the first string. The other strings are represented by the lines in descending order as shown below.

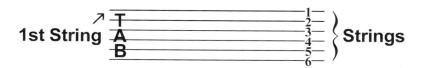

A number on a line indicates in which fret to place a left-hand finger.

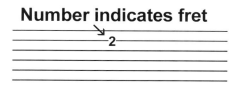

In the example below, the finger would be placed on the first string in the third fret.

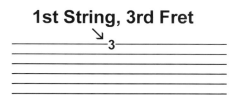

If two or more numbers are written on top of one another, play the strings at the same time.

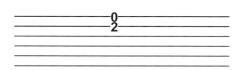

# Building the Blues

The chords most commonly used in the blues are the I, IV, and V chords. The Roman numeral I is used to represent the key of the song. For example, the I in the key of A is A. The IV chord is four steps up the major scale (usually four names up the alphabet) from the I chord. For example, the IV chord in the key of A is D. The V chord is five steps up the major scale (alphabet) from the I chord. The V chord in the key of A is E. Seventh (7) chords are commonly used for every chord in the blues. Seventh chords are used because they have a dissonant, off-key sound to them. This dissonance reflects how one might feel when having the blues.

The chart below lists the I, IV, and V chords in some of the basic keys. By learning the blues progression using Roman numerals, the correct chords may be inserted and the blues can be played in any key.

|  | I | IV | V |
|---|---|---|---|
| **Easiest keys for open chords** | C7 | F7 | G7 |
|  | G7 | C7 | D7 |
|  | D7 | G7 | A7 |
|  | A7 | D7 | E7 |
|  | E7 | A7 | B7 |
| **Keys using moveable chords** | B7 | E7 | F♯7 |
|  | F♯7 | B7 | C♯7 |
|  | D♭7 | G♭7 | A♭7 |
|  | A♭7 | D♭7 | E♭7 |
|  | E♭7 | A♭7 | B♭7 |
|  | B♭7 | E♭7 | F7 |
|  | F7 | B♭7 | C7 |

The formula for constructing the standard 12-bar blues progression is: one measure of the I chord, one measure of the IV chord, two measures of the I chord, two measures of the IV chord, two measures of the I chord, one measure of the V chord, one measure of the IV chord, and two measures of the I chord. This basic progression, with some variations, is used throughout this book.

# Strum Patterns

A strum pattern can be used to create interest to the accompaniment. A strum pattern can consist of a combination of down and up strums. A down-strum is indicated with this sign, ⊓, written above the strum bar. The up strum is indicated with this sign, V, written above the strum bar. Regardless of the chord being played, when doing an up-strum, only the first (highest sounding) three or four strings should be strummed. The pick should be used and angled downward slightly when doing the up-strum. When two strums are connected with a beam, ⊓ᵥ, they are called eighth note strums. When playing eighth-note strums, there are two notes played in one beat. The first strum bar is a downstroke and is played on the first half of the beat. The up-strum is played on the second half of the beat. The eighth-note strum is the strum equivalent to eighth notes in standard notation. The downstroke is counted as the number of the beat on which it occurs, and the up strum is counted as "and," example:

Very often, eighth-note strums ( ⊓ᵥ ) are played using **swing rhythm.** In swing rhythm, rather than the beat being divided into two equal parts, the down-strum gets about two-thirds of the beat and the up-strum gets the remaining one-third of the beat.

If playing with swing rhythm is difficult at first, think of the melody to "Battle Hymn of the Republic." This melody is often sung with swing rhythm. If a piece of music is to be played using swing rhythm, sometimes this, ( ♪♪ = ♪ᶾ♪ ) will be written at the beginning of the music. Practice the following exercise playing the down and up strums evenly. Then, repeat the exercise using swing rhythm.

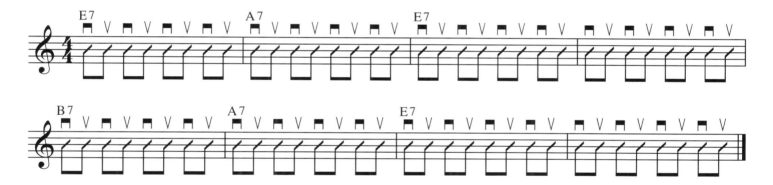

Written below are six strum patterns which are commonly used to play the blues. Each of the strum patterns take one measure of 4/4 to complete and can be used to play any blues song in 4/4. Once a pattern has been selected, play the same pattern in each measure of the piece. It is uncommon to combine patterns.

Practice holding any chord and play each pattern. Be careful to use the correct strum direction and correct rhythm. Tap your foot on each beat and count the rhythms aloud. The patterns are written in order of difficulty. Master one pattern before moving to the next.

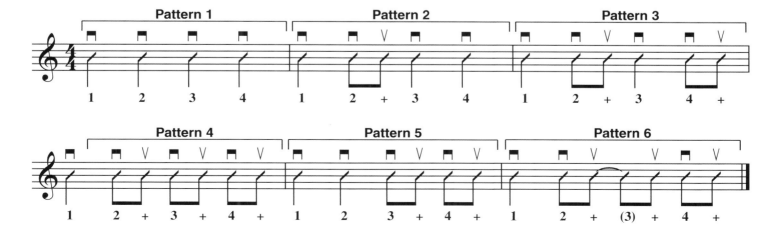

# Fingerstyle Accompaniment

Fingerstyle accompaniment can be a very important aspect of playing blues guitar. Blues guitar legends like Robert Johnson and Rev. Gary Davis all have used fingerpicking patterns to give their guitar accompaniment a unique sound. The following fingerpicking patterns are to be applied to six-string, five-string, and four-string chords just as the alternating bass patterns. When applying these patterns, simply determine how many strings the chord being played uses and apply the pattern. When starting this type of accompaniment, it is suggested that one pattern (for each of the three chord types) be selected and played for the entire tune. After many patterns have been mastered, one can mix and match the patterns for a more spontaneous sound.

The following pattern will help guitarists coordinate the fingers of the right hand and prepare them for more involved patterns to follow.

① 4/4

| | 6-String Chords | | | | | | | | 5-String Chords | | | | | | | | 4-String Chords | | | | | | |
|---|---|---|---|---|---|---|---|---|---|---|---|---|---|---|---|---|---|---|---|---|---|---|---|
| | 6 | 2 | 4 | 3 | 6 | 2 | 4 | 3 | 5 | 2 | 4 | 3 | 5 | 2 | 4 | 3 | 4 | 1 | 3 | 2 | 4 | 1 | 3 | 2 |
| Fingering: | p | m | p | i | p | m | p | i | p | m | p | i | p | m | p | i | p | m | p | i | p | m | p | i |
| Rhythm: | 1 | & | 2 | & | 3 | & | 4 | & | 1 | & | 2 | & | 3 | & | 4 | & | 1 | & | 2 | & | 3 | & | 4 | & |

Remember, right hand: *p* = thumb, *i* = index finger, *m* = middle finger, and *a* = ring finger.

The next patterns work well over progressions and tunes in 4/4 and 3/4. Apply these patterns to the chord progressions in this book. Feel free to use different patterns over each of the chord progressions for practicing purposes. The goal should be to apply all of the accompaniment patterns presented in a variety of ways and over a variety of tunes. Holding G, C, and D chords, practice each of the following fingerpicking patterns.

② 4/4

| | 6-String Chords | | | | | | | | 5-String Chords | | | | | | | | 4-String Chords | | | | | | |
|---|---|---|---|---|---|---|---|---|---|---|---|---|---|---|---|---|---|---|---|---|---|---|---|---|
| | 6 | – | 4 | 3 | 6 | 2 | 4 | 3 | 5 | – | 4 | 3 | 5 | 2 | 4 | 3 | 4 | – | 3 | 2 | 4 | 1 | 3 | 2 |
| | p | | p | i | p | m | p | i | p | | p | i | p | m | p | i | p | | p | i | p | m | p | i |
| | 1 | | 2 | & | 3 | & | 4 | & | 1 | | 2 | & | 3 | & | 4 | & | 1 | | 2 | & | 3 | & | 4 | & |

③ 4/4

| | 6-String Chords | | | | | | | | 5-String Chords | | | | | | | | 4-String Chords | | | | | | |
|---|---|---|---|---|---|---|---|---|---|---|---|---|---|---|---|---|---|---|---|---|---|---|---|---|
| | 6 | 4 | 3 | 2 | 6 | 4 | 3 | 2 | 5 | 4 | 3 | 2 | 5 | 4 | 3 | 2 | 4 | 3 | 2 | 1 | 4 | 3 | 2 | 1 |
| | p | p | i | m | p | p | i | m | p | p | i | m | p | p | i | m | p | p | i | m | p | p | i | m |
| | 1 | & | 2 | & | 3 | & | 4 | & | 1 | & | 2 | & | 3 | & | 4 | & | 1 | & | 2 | & | 3 | & | 4 | & |

④ 3/4

| | 6-String Chords | | | | | | 5-String Chords | | | | | | 4-String Chords | | | | | |
|---|---|---|---|---|---|---|---|---|---|---|---|---|---|---|---|---|---|---|
| | 6 | 4 | 3 | 2 | 4 | 3 | 5 | 4 | 3 | 2 | 4 | 3 | 4 | 3 | 2 | 1 | 3 | 2 |
| | p | p | i | m | p | i | p | p | i | m | p | i | p | p | i | m | p | i |
| | 1 | & | 2 | & | 3 | & | 1 | & | 2 | & | 3 | & | 1 | & | 2 | & | 3 | & |

Two notes can be plucked simultaneously to add a rich, full sound to any of the above patterns. Here are a few examples of this technique. Try creating original patterns that make use of two notes being played at once. Remember to repeat the patterns making the appropriate adjustments for each of the three chord types. Many guitarists will use the high pitched extra note (when two notes are played at one time) to accentuate the melody of a tune. It is nice to play a melody note, when appropriate and playable, in the accompaniment.

### ⑤ 4/4

**6-String Chords**

| Extra | | | | | | | |
|---|---|---|---|---|---|---|---|
| 1 | | | | | | | |
| 6 | – | 4 | 3 | 6 | 2 | 4 | 3 |
| m | | | | | | | |
| p | | p | i | p | m | p | i |
| 1 | | 2 | & | 3 | & | 4 | & |

**5-String Chords**

| 1 | | | | | | | |
|---|---|---|---|---|---|---|---|
| 5 | – | 4 | 3 | 5 | 2 | 4 | 3 |
| m | | | | | | | |
| p | | p | i | p | m | p | i |
| 1 | | 2 | & | 3 | & | 4 | & |

**4-String Chords**

| 1 | | | | | | | |
|---|---|---|---|---|---|---|---|
| 4 | – | 3 | 2 | 4 | 1 | 3 | 2 |
| m | | | | | | | |
| p | | p | i | p | m | p | i |
| 1 | | 2 | & | 3 | & | 4 | & |

### ⑥ 4/4

**6-String Chords**

| 1 | | | | | | | |
|---|---|---|---|---|---|---|---|
| 6 | – | 4 | – | 6 | 2 | 4 | 3 |
| | | m | | | | | |
| p | | p | | p | m | p | i |
| 1 | | 2 | | 3 | & | 4 | & |

**5-String Chords**

| 1 | | | | | | | |
|---|---|---|---|---|---|---|---|
| 5 | – | 4 | – | 5 | 2 | 4 | 3 |
| | | m | | | | | |
| p | | p | | p | m | p | i |
| 1 | | 2 | | 3 | & | 4 | & |

**4-String Chords**

| 1 | | | | | | | |
|---|---|---|---|---|---|---|---|
| 4 | – | 3 | – | 4 | 1 | 3 | 2 |
| | | m | | | | | |
| p | | p | | p | m | p | i |
| 1 | | 2 | | 3 | & | 4 | & |

### ⑦ 4/4

**6-String Chords**

| 1 | | | | | | | |
|---|---|---|---|---|---|---|---|
| 6 | 4 | 3 | 2 | 6 | 4 | 3 | 2 |
| m | | | | | | | |
| p | p | i | m | p | p | i | m |
| 1 | & | 2 | & | 3 | & | 4 | & |

**5-String Chords**

| 1 | | | | | | | |
|---|---|---|---|---|---|---|---|
| 5 | 4 | 3 | 2 | 5 | 4 | 3 | 2 |
| m | | | | | | | |
| p | p | i | m | p | p | i | m |
| 1 | & | 2 | & | 3 | & | 4 | & |

**4-String Chords**

| 1 | | | | | | | |
|---|---|---|---|---|---|---|---|
| 4 | 3 | 2 | 1 | 4 | 3 | 2 | 1 |
| m | | | | | | | |
| p | p | i | m | p | p | i | m |
| 1 | & | 2 | & | 3 | & | 4 | & |

### ⑧ 4/4

**6-String Chords**

| | | 2 | | | | 2 | |
|---|---|---|---|---|---|---|---|
| 6 | 4 | 3 | 4 | 6 | 4 | 3 | 4 |
| | | m | | | | m | |
| p | p | i | p | p | p | i | p |
| 1 | & | 2 | & | 3 | & | 4 | & |

**5-String Chords**

| | | 2 | | | | 2 | |
|---|---|---|---|---|---|---|---|
| 5 | 4 | 3 | 4 | 5 | 4 | 3 | 4 |
| | | m | | | | m | |
| p | p | i | p | p | p | i | p |
| 1 | & | 2 | & | 3 | & | 4 | & |

**4-String Chords**

| | | 1 | | | | 1 | |
|---|---|---|---|---|---|---|---|
| 4 | 3 | 2 | 3 | 4 | 3 | 2 | 4 |
| | | m | | | | m | |
| p | p | i | p | p | p | i | p |
| 1 | & | 2 | & | 3 | & | 4 | & |

### ⑨ 3/4

**6-String Chords**

| 1 | | | | | |
|---|---|---|---|---|---|
| 6 | 4 | 3 | 2 | 4 | 3 |
| m | | | | | |
| p | p | i | m | p | i |
| 1 | & | 2 | & | 3 | & |

**5-String Chords**

| 1 | | | | | |
|---|---|---|---|---|---|
| 5 | 4 | 3 | 2 | 4 | 3 |
| m | | | | | |
| p | p | i | m | p | i |
| 1 | & | 2 | & | 3 | & |

**4-String Chords**

| 1 | | | | | |
|---|---|---|---|---|---|
| 4 | 3 | 2 | 1 | 3 | 2 |
| m | | | | | |
| p | p | i | m | p | i |
| 1 | & | 2 | & | 3 | & |

### ⑩ 3/4

**6-String Chords**

| | | 2 | | 2 | |
|---|---|---|---|---|---|
| 6 | 4 | 3 | 4 | 3 | 4 |
| | | m | | m | |
| p | p | i | p | i | p |
| 1 | & | 2 | & | 3 | & |

**5-String Chords**

| | | 2 | | 2 | |
|---|---|---|---|---|---|
| 5 | 4 | 3 | 4 | 3 | 4 |
| | | m | | m | |
| p | p | i | p | i | p |
| 1 | & | 2 | & | 3 | & |

**4-String Chords**

| | | 1 | | 1 | |
|---|---|---|---|---|---|
| 4 | 3 | 2 | 3 | 2 | 3 |
| | | m | | m | |
| p | p | i | p | i | p |
| 1 | & | 2 | & | 3 | & |

# Open Chords

Open chords are the most commonly used chords in the world. They are used in virtually every style of music. They are called open chords because they utilize open strings (strings that are not fingered). Most of these types of chords are in first position. This means that the first four frets of the guitar (and mostly just the first three frets) are used to execute these chords.

# A Blues Open Chords

The three chords used in a blues in the key of A are A7, D7 and E7.

**A 7**

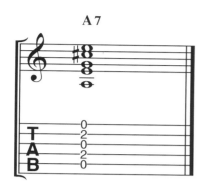

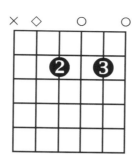

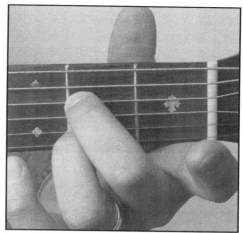

**D 7**

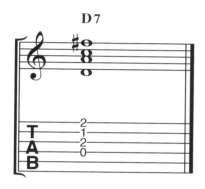

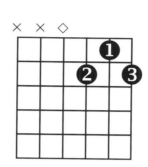

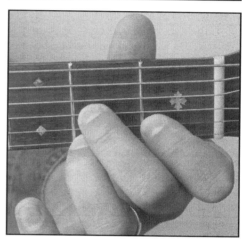

**E 7**

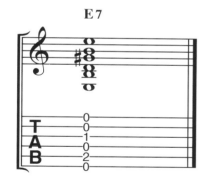

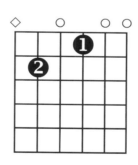

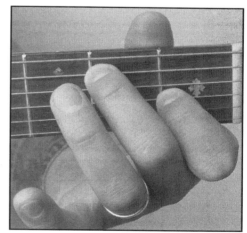

**E 7**

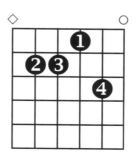

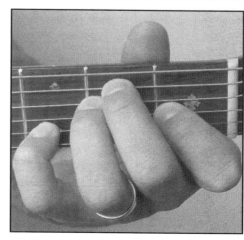

12

The following chord progression is a 12-bar blues in the key of A. Simply use the shapes provided for the following chords. Simply use any strumming pattern (p.7-9) that will work for 4/4 time.

# E Blues Open Chords

The chords for a blues in the key of E are E7 and B7. Only one new chord is needed to play a blues with open chords in the key of E when you know the chords for a blues in the key of A. That chord is B7.

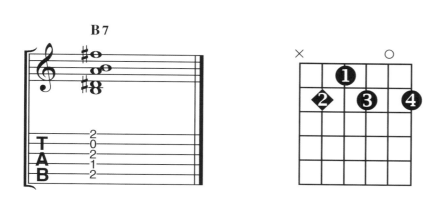

The following chord progression is a 12 bar blues in the key of E.

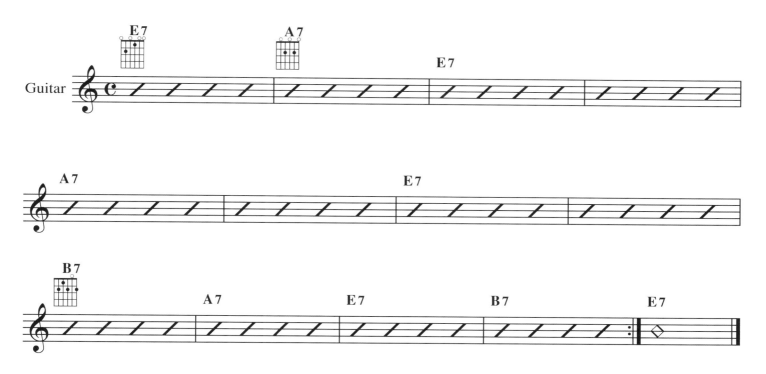

Note: Remember to apply one of the strum or fingerpicking patterns to this progression.

# D Blues Open Chords

The chords in a D blues are D7, G7, and A7. G7 is the only new chord needed to play blues in the key of D.

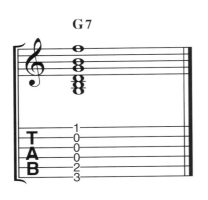
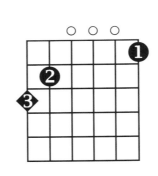
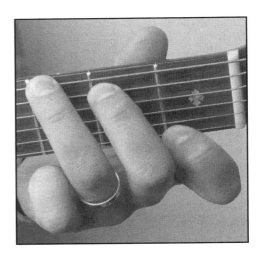

This is a blues in the key of D.

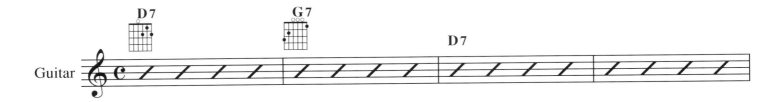

Note: Remember to apply one of the strum or fingerpicking patterns to this progression.

# G Blues Open Chords

The chords in a G blues are G7, C7 and D7. C7 is the only new chord needed to play a blues in the key of G.

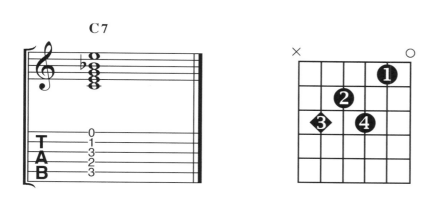

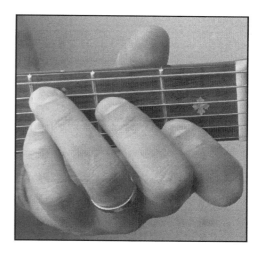

A blues in the key of G is found below.

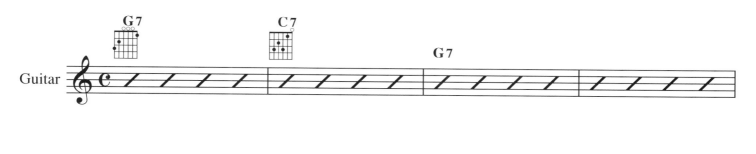

Note: Remember to apply one of the strum or fingerpicking patterns to this progression.

# Open Minor Chords

**A m**

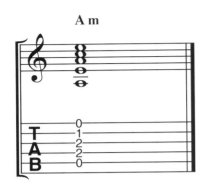
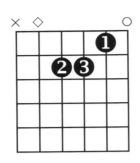

**A m7**

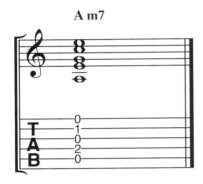
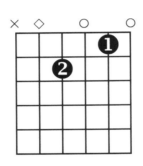
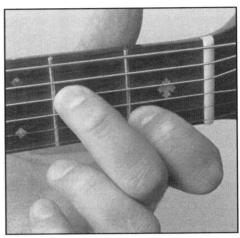

**A m7**

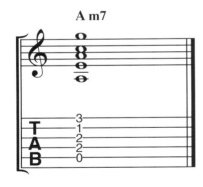
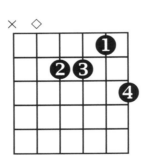

**D m**

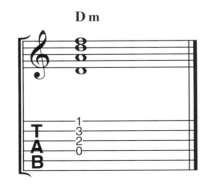
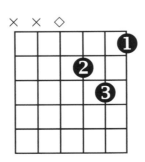

**D m7**

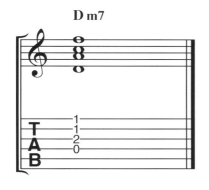
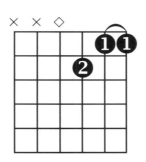
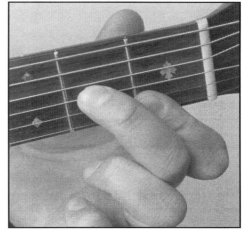

**E m**

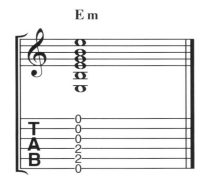
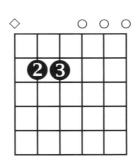
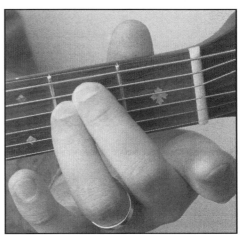

**E m7**

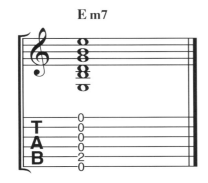
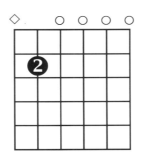
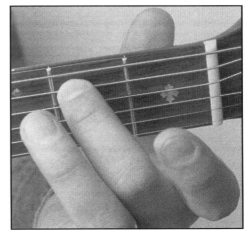

**E m7**

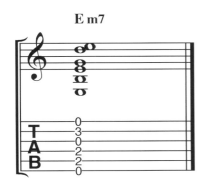
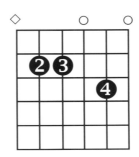
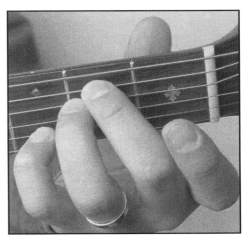

# Minor Blues

When playing the blues in a minor key, the Roman numeral formula can still be used, but the i and iv chords become minor and are represented by small Roman numerals. The V chord remains a seventh chord. Written below is a minor blues in the key of A minor. Practice strumming this progression using one of the strum patterns for 4/4.

Practice the following blues in the key of A minor.

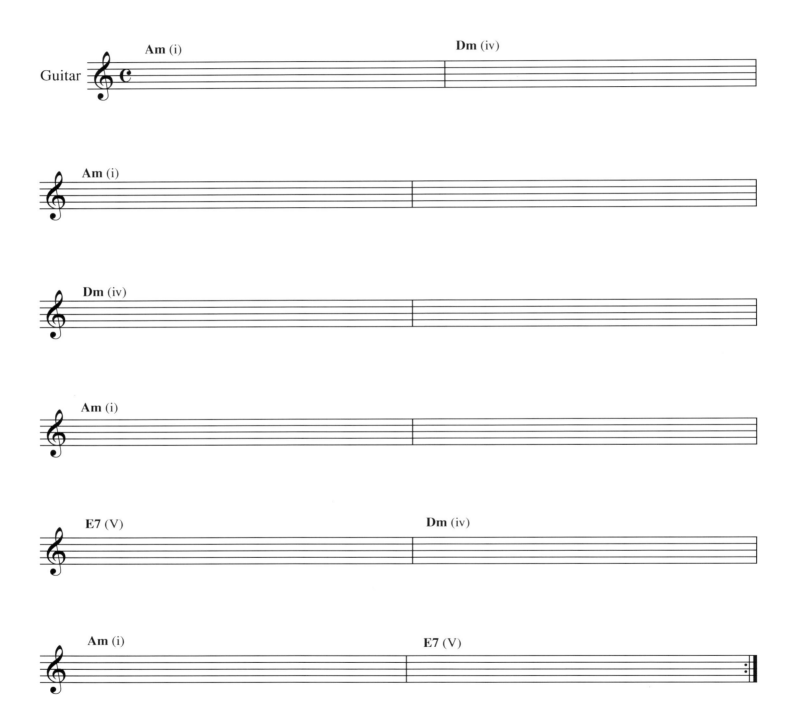

The next blues is in the key of E minor. Usually a minor seventh (m7) chord can replace any other minor chord in the blues. Experiment with the minor and m7 chords previously shown.

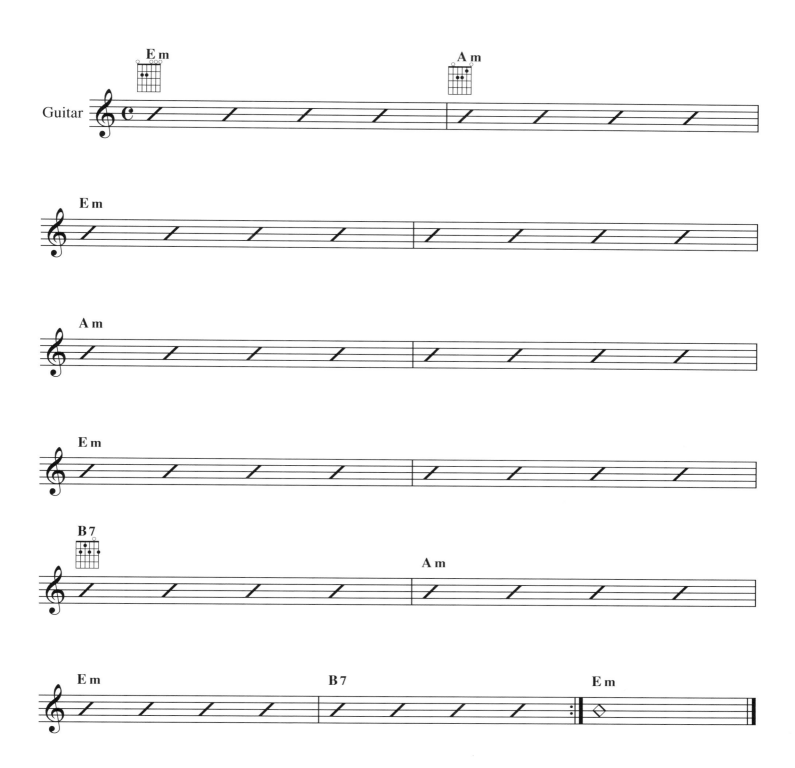

Note: Remember to apply one of the strum or fingerpicking patterns to this progression.

# Open Power Chords

Power chords are heavy sounding chords that are easily played but work great in many settings. They are most commonly referred to as "5" chords. Therefore E5 is the same as saying, "E power chord." They can replace major, minor, 7, and m7 chords as well as any other chord unless the fifth of the chord is altered ($\sharp$5, $\flat$5)

**E5**

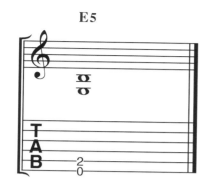
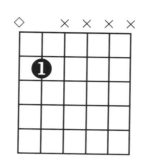
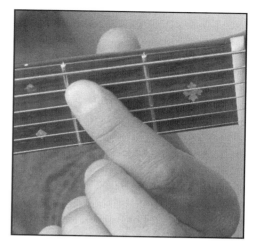

**E5**

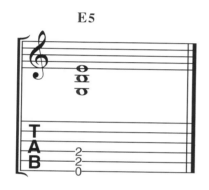
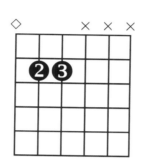
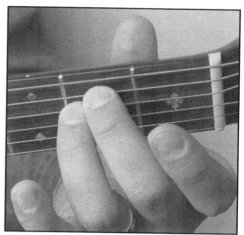

**A5**

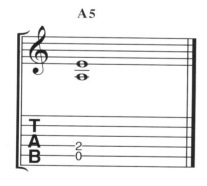
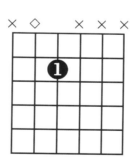
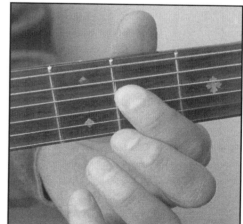

**A5**

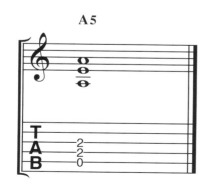
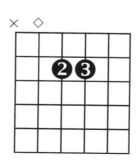
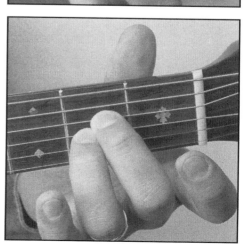

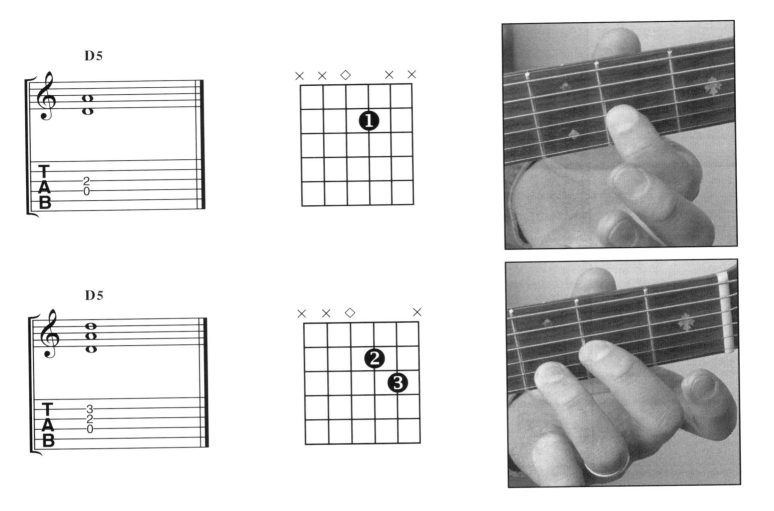

This blues in the key of A uses open power chords.

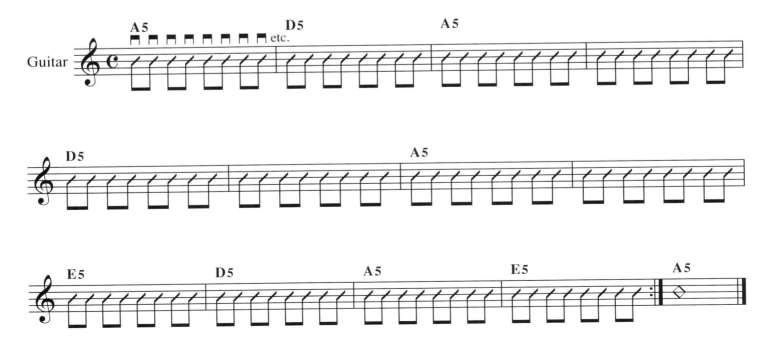

A common variation on the power chord involves adding a finger on the third and seventh down-strokes (on the second and fourth beats) of the measure. For example, on the A5 chord, play strings 5 and 4 together four times. Use only down-strokes. On the third stroke, add the left-hand third finger where the "3" is drawn on the diagram below. On the fourth stroke, lift the third finger. Do this twice in each measure.

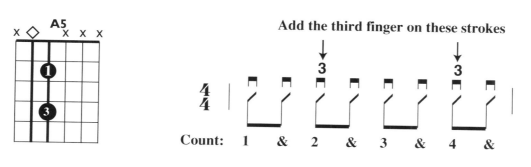

This technique could be used on the D5 chord by adding the third finger on the third string where the "3" is drawn.

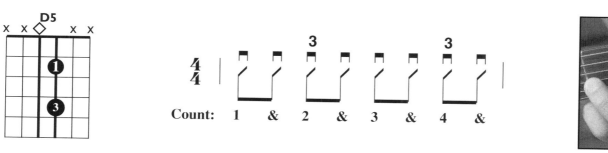

For the E5, add the third finger in the fourth fret on the fifth string.

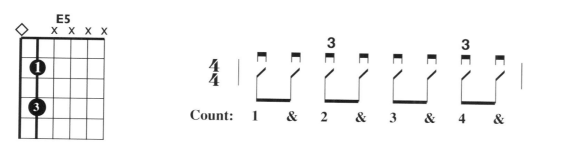

Play this twelve-bar blues which uses the variations on the power chord.

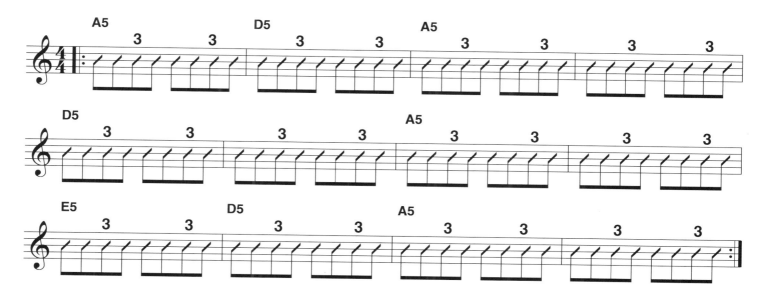

# Root Notes and Moveable Chord Shapes

Many of the chords presented in this book are moveable. This means that the shapes can be moved to create a different chord name. For example a G power chord moved up two frets becomes an A power chord. All one has to know is where the root(the note that names the chord) is located within the shape and where all of the notes are on the fingerboard. The following charts show where all of the natural notes are on the guitar fingerboard. The sixth and first string have the same fret and note name relationship; they are just two octaves apart. Remember to sharp (♯) a note, raise it one fret. This means to move it one fret closer to the body of the guitar. To flat (♭) a note, lower it one fret. This means to move it one fret towards the head the guitar. Ok, now every moveable chord shape presented can be played in all 12 keys.

### Root Notes On The Sixth and First String

| 0 | 1 | 3 | 5 | 7 | 8 | 10 | 12 |
|---|---|---|---|---|---|----|----|
| E | F | G | A | B | C | D  | E  |

### Root Notes On The Fifth String

| 0 | 2 | 3 | 5 | 7 | 8 | 10 | 12 |
|---|---|---|---|---|---|----|----|
| A | B | C | D | E | F | G  | A  |

### Root Notes On The Fourth String

| 0 | 2 | 3 | 5 | 7 | 9 | 10 | 12 |
|---|---|---|---|---|---|----|----|
| D | E | F | G | A | B | C  | D  |

### Root Notes On The Third String

| 0 | 2 | 4 | 5 | 7 | 9 | 10 | 12 |
|---|---|---|---|---|---|----|----|
| G | A | B | C | D | E | F  | G  |

### Root Notes On Second String

| 0 | 1 | 3 | 5 | 6 | 8 | 10 | 12 |
|---|---|---|---|---|---|----|----|
| B | C | D | E | F | G | A  | B  |

# Moveable Power Chords

Moveable power chords are usually lumped into a few groups. The first group are shapes based off the root note (note that names the chord) on the sixth string. The second is based off shapes with the root on the fifth string and the third group is based off shapes with the root on the fourth string. Whatever fret the root note is placed will determine the name of the chord. Diagrams showing the root notes on the sixth, fifth and fourth strings are found below. Remember to flat (♭) a note, lower it (move it closer to the headstock of the guitar) by one fret. To sharp (♯) a note, raise it (move it closer to the body of the guitar) by one fret. Be sure to practice these chords in all twelve keys. Notice there are three shapes for these chords. One has the root on the lowest sounding string, one has two root notes, and the other has the root on the highest sounding string.

# Moveable Power Chords

**A5**

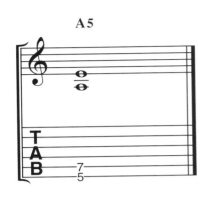

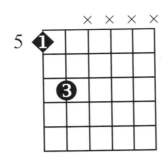

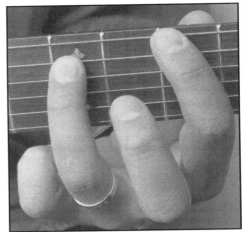

**A5**

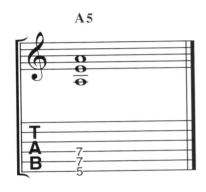

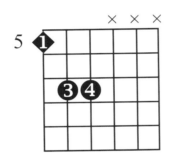

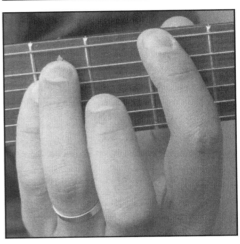

**A5**

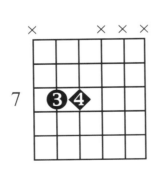

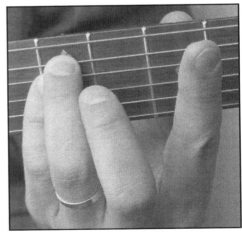

**D5**

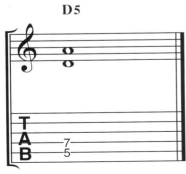

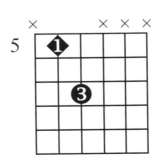

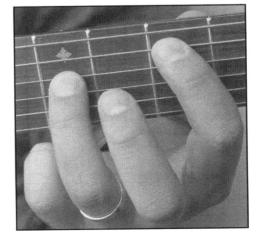

Note: the chords on this page are moveable and can be played in any of the twelve keys. See page 24 for more information.

**D5**

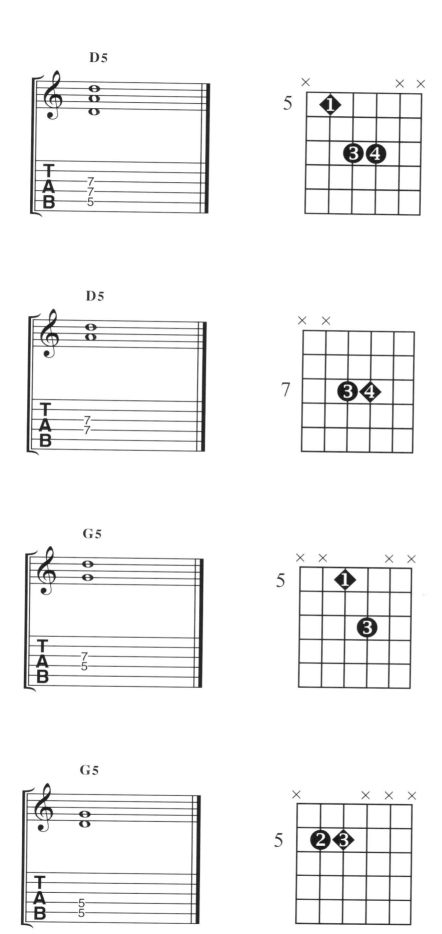

**D5**

**G5**

**G5**

Note: the chords on this page are moveable and can be played
in any of the twelve keys. See page 24 for more information.

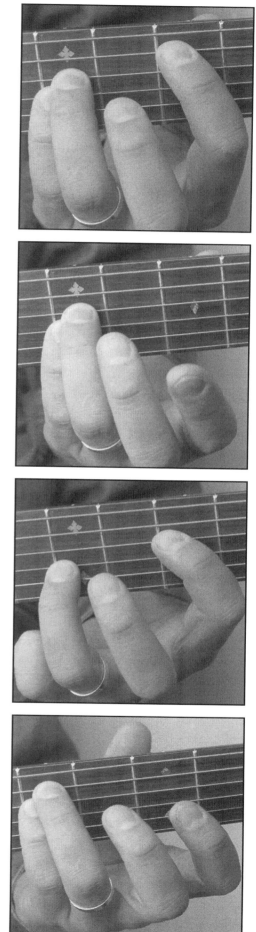

# Barre Chords

Like power chords, barre chords are moveable shapes. They are called barre chords because at least one finger is used to press down more than one string at a time. The following chords have their roots on the sixth string and the fifth string.

Be sure to go back and play some of the previously presented blues progressions with barre chords.

**Root on 6th String**

**G Major**

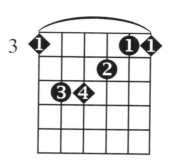

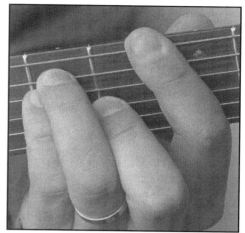

**G m**

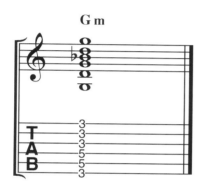

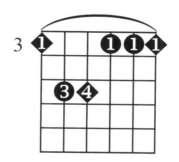

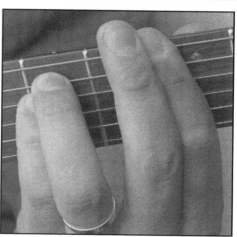

**G 7**

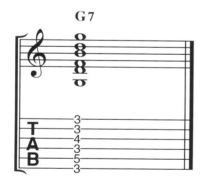

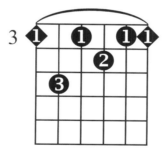

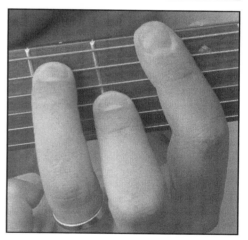

Note: the chords on this page are moveable and can be played in any of the twelve keys. See page 24 for more information.

**G m7**

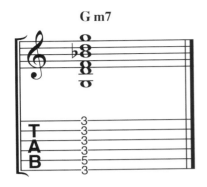 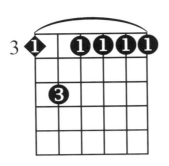 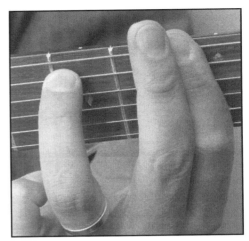

**G m7**

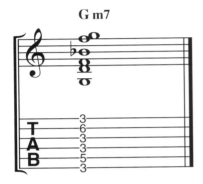 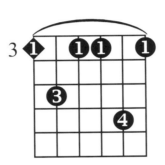 

Note: the chords on this page are moveable and can be played
in any of the twelve keys. See page 24 for more information.

# 5th String Barre Chords

**Root on 5th String**

**C**

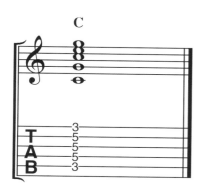
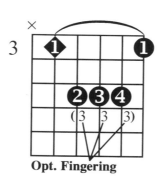
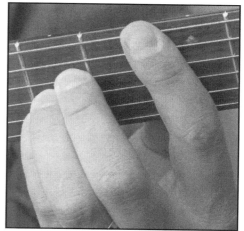

**Opt. Fingering**

**C m**

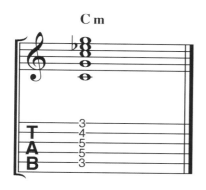
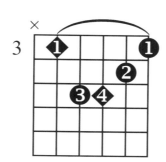
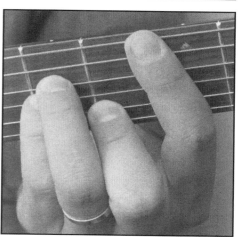

**C 7**

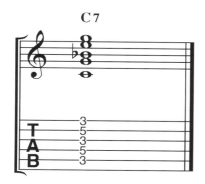
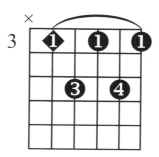
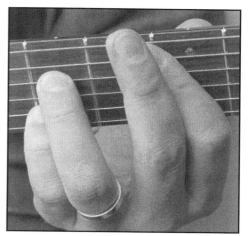

**C m7**

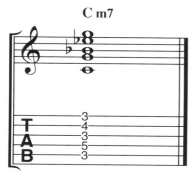
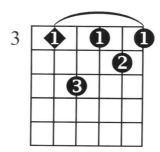
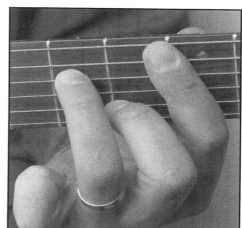

Note: the chords on this page are moveable and can be played in any of the twelve keys. See page 24 for more information.

# Moveable Four-String Chords

Four-string chords can be used in a variety of settings. They are the perfect choice when a lighter sound is desired. They also work great when playing with another guitarist. Rather than doubling the exact same G chord in open position, for example, the four-string chord with the same name can be used. It creates the sound of a much larger chord. Groups with more than one guitar have used this concept to create some wonderful guitar orchestrations.

Notice that some of the chords are written with a slash. This means that a note other than the root note is in the lowest position. This is called an inversion. It is still the same chord, just a different organization or order of the notes. These chords really do sound great. All of these chords are presented with G as the root note. Be sure to practice these in many other keys as well.

These voicings work great when playing blues with a band. Try to use shapes that lead well into each other. The possibilities are quite vast with these chords. They can yield a more sophisticated sound.

Each chord is presented with at least two inversions. Remember, inversions occur when a chord tone other than the root is located in the lowest voice. An inverted chord is written as a chord symbol, followed by a slash and a bass note (G/B). In the case of G/B, the chord symbol is read as G with a B in the bass. Not all slash chords are inversions. If the note in the bass is not a chord tone, they would be considered chords with added bass notes.

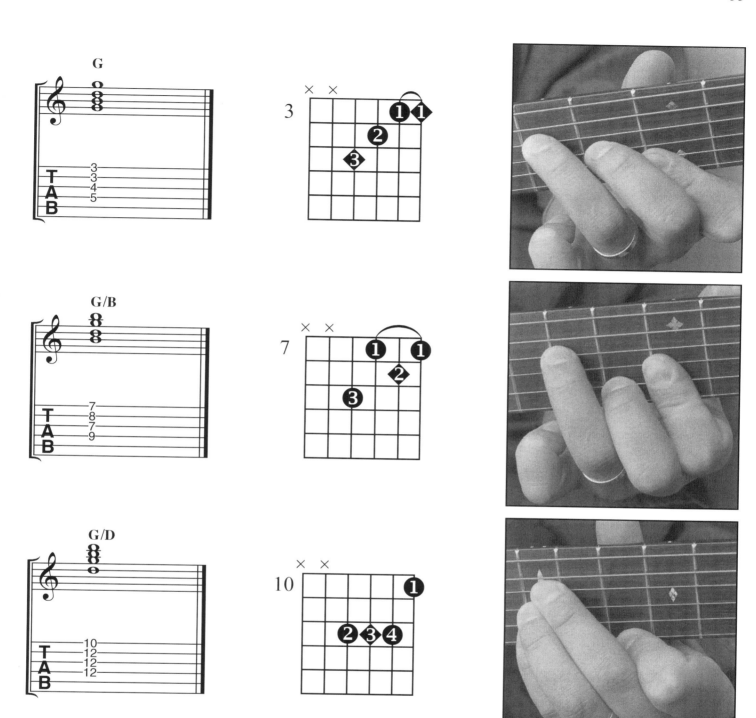

Note: the chords on this page are moveable and can be played
in any of the twelve keys. See page 24 for more information.

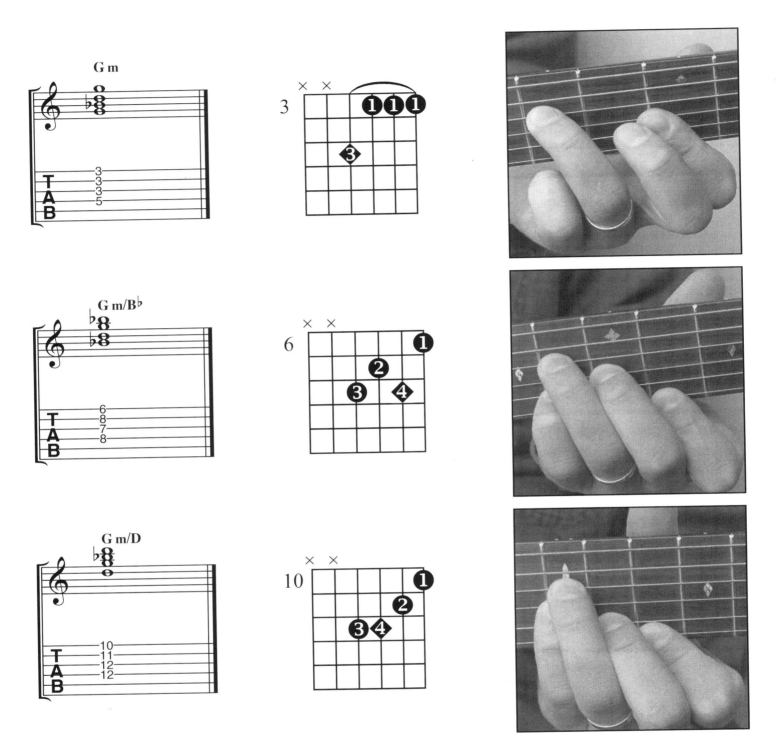

**G m**

**G m/B♭**

**G m/D**

Note: the chords on this page are moveable and can be played
in any of the twelve keys. See page 24 for more information.

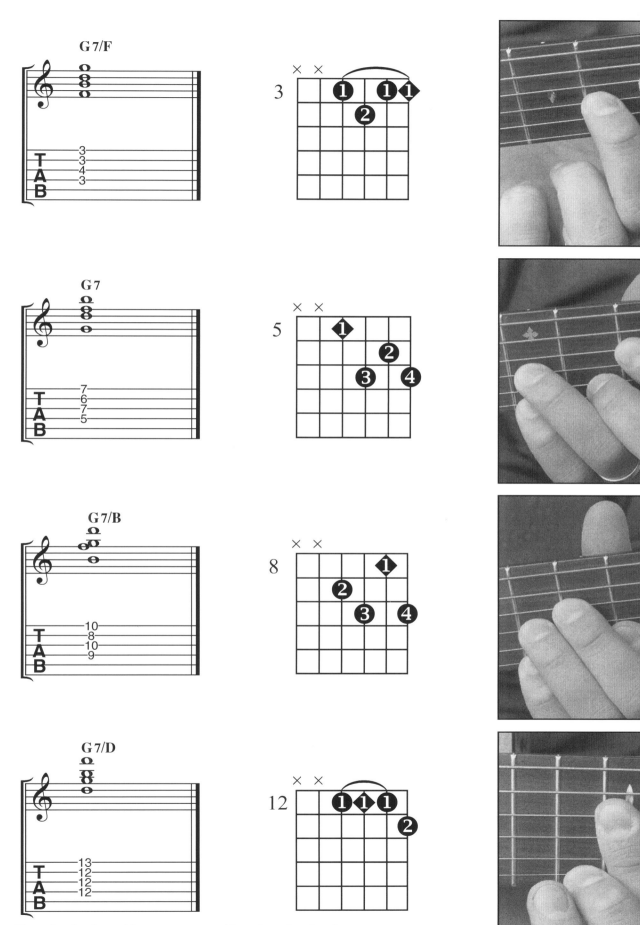

Note: the chords on this page are moveable and can be played in any of the twelve keys. See page 24 for more information.

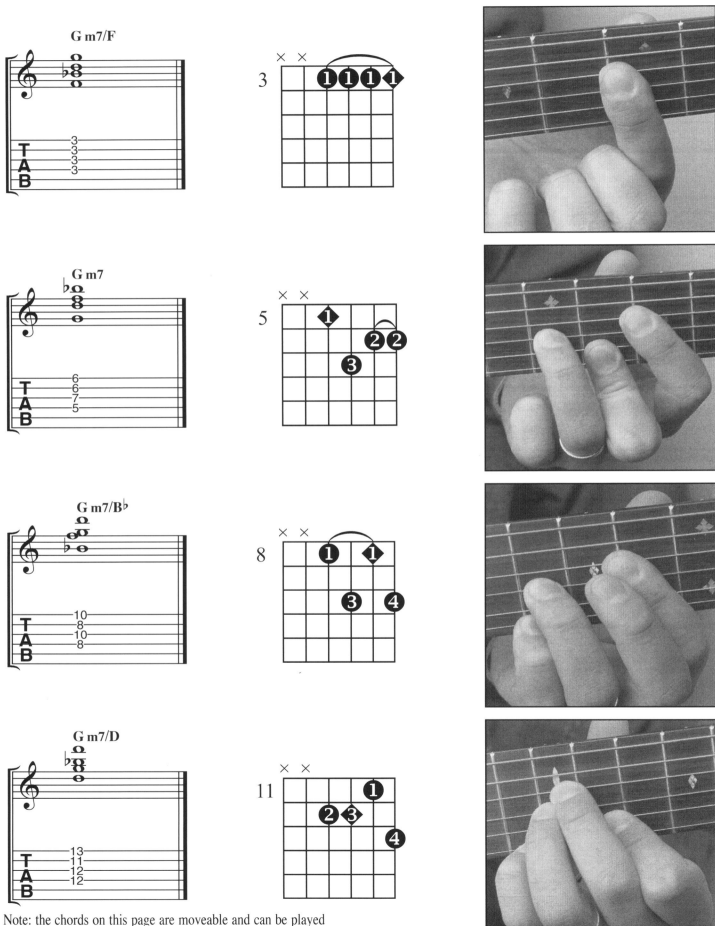

**G m7/F**

3

**G m7**

5

**G m7/B♭**

8

**G m7/D**

11

Note: the chords on this page are moveable and can be played in any of the twelve keys. See page 24 for more information.

# Four String Blues in G

Use the following chord shapes below to play this blues using four-string chords. Notice that the inversions (bass notes) are not labeled. This shows that really any inversion of a chord can be used as long as it leads well to the the next chord.

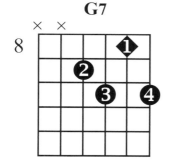

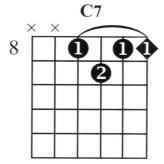

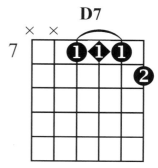

Note: Remember to apply one of the strum or fingerpicking patterns to this progression.

# Four String Blues in B♭

Here's another blues using four-string chords. This one is in the key of B♭.

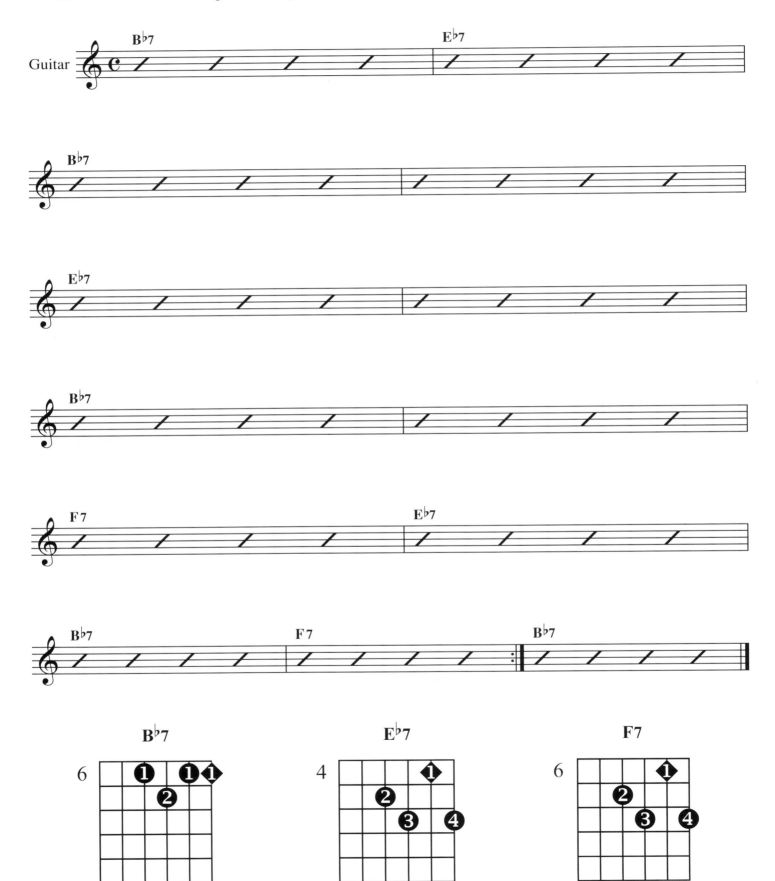

# Appendix
## Extra Blues Progressions

Use all of the following blues with the chords that have been presented in this book. Feel free to experiment with different voicings and chord types. Most of all have fun.